Vanora

E D Skinner

ISBN-13:   978-1-963180-03-9 Paperback

978-1-963180-02-2 Ebook

A cold, wet draft made Gil Watson close his eyes and hunch his chin inside the heavy collar. The fabric chafed but held its shape from the crudeness of its weave.

"Slut!" a voice barked in front of him.

Gil opened his eyes.

Five paces out on the stone-paved floor, a short, red-faced man stood with bunched fists on hips amidst a mess of tables and half-eaten food. Rust speckled his chain mail above mud-streaked leather boots. Deep lines struck across his forehead and bracketed his frown, but his eyes burnt with an unmistakable and deadly hatred.

A step behind him, four others in similar armor waited, their expressions also hard, committed, and ready for battle. All five wore white tunics with a large red cross atop their armor. Each person wore a leather belt with a sword scabbard around their waist. The four in the back had plain metal hilts, while the man in front had a silver hilt with red and blue jewels.

Gil ran a hand up to his forehead, the black stone in his silver ring glinting with the fire. He brushed back what he thought would be a loose wisp of grey hair but discovered instead the jet-black mop of his youth. He patted its thick waviness, reveling again, after so many years, at its sensuality.

A melodious woman's voice came from Gil's left. "My dear Arthur, you have us at a loss, your return—premature?—so soon."

Gil turned his head to look, and his mouth crept open.

Cascading tresses of coppery-red hair tied back with opalescent white pearls swirled around her head. She had a long, straight nose, a prominent chin, and high cheekbones like some Roman statue. Her pale and glowing complexion bested the oyster baubles in her hair. Dressed in a full-length blue gown under a red jacket with embroidered white lace, she sat on an elegantly carved wood throne on a red pillow with silver tassels.

Her blue-green eyes flared at the filthy entourage in front of them.

"Alas," she said, putting a hand to her nose, "the proof of your haste befouls the room. Pray, move to the hearth so it may draw away the evidence."

1

Gil lifted a hand to hide his amusement. He liked this woman's spunk.

He shifted in his seat and noticed he was sitting on a royal purple pillow with gold thread, and on a slightly taller wooden throne.

The armored man sneered at the woman. "Foul bitch. Castle whore. Polecat of bedchambers."

Gil felt his ears and face burn at the gruff man's insults. He tensed to rise, but a hand fell on his arm and squeezed.

"Ah, poor Arthur," the woman lilted as if she were singing. "I see your encounters with the Roman Emperor have failed to improve your vocabulary. That is—"

"I am your husband," the man bellowed. "I am your King. Bow down!"

King Arthur! Gil realized. And the woman he accused, the one with her hand on Gil's arm, must be Guinevere.

The most beautiful woman in England, he remembered reading years ago.

A large, gray Deerhound, its chest filling Gil's lap with hind feet on the floor, turned its enormous head and growled at the intruders.

"Easy, Tavish," Gil heard himself say as he smiled and smoothed the hackles along the dog's spine.

Gil's smile was his best and only attractive feature. Round nose, round eyes, round face—his entire physique invited the same description. But when the corners of his mouth raised, women smiled, and men cooled.

But not this man.

Arthur shifted a chain-mailed hand to the hilt of his sword.

The motion drew Gil's eyes to the scabbard. It was short, no more than two feet long, much too short for Excalibur. This had to be a Roman soldier's blade, captured or taken from a dead man in some battle, perhaps, then decorated for a king.

It reminded Gil of the gaudy ones discounted on the last afternoon at one of Clarissa's Renaissance festivals.

Clarissa, Gil's mind echoed. *My wife. She's dead.*

Arthur's sword flashed as it came from the scabbard, and he

bolted forward.

In a gasp, his knights followed as all five of them leapt onto the head table in front of Gil and Guinevere. The wood creaked from their sudden weight, and the attackers tottered a moment, unsure of their footing.

"Come!" Guinevere shouted as she yanked Gil up. Tavish yelped as he tumbled to the main floor and scrambled with his long legs to regain his footing.

Pulling Gil with her, Guinevere leapt down from the rear of their platform, shoved aside a heavy tapestry, and plunged into an unlit passage. They ran only a few steps before the tapestry closed, enveloping them in darkness. Gil dragged her to a stop, his other hand searching for a wall.

"No," she hissed and kept pulling. "This way!"

"Wake up, sir," a woman said. "We're landing in Edinburgh."

Gil rubbed his eyes and gazed out the window, but thick, dark clouds surrounded the plane.

Strange dream, he thought. *I understood what they were saying, but in real life, their language—was that Gaelic?—would be gibberish.*

Outside the airplane, lightning flashed, and a bolt of pain shot up Gil's left arm.

Muscle spasm, he rationalized again. The pain in that arm and shoulder had started after Clarissa's passing. They seemed to spike up with Indiana's storms. He knew he should see a doctor, but with her gone, there was no point. The church had given him a deal at her burial, but the memorial stone was too much. He knew where to find it, and it's not as though anyone else would come to visit.

He'd sold their house to pay off both mortgages. The rest went for his ticket to Scotland, a lifelong, and now life-ending, dream.

"The Watsons hail from there," his dad had told him decades ago. "A place called *Lang Logie*."

He'd dreamed of going all his life, but they'd never had the money or the time. They'd stayed together, living their separate lives, his one indiscretion forever standing between them. He'd failed her in a fit of anger once, decades ago, and it'd kept them apart but locked together with nowhere to go, no other life to live.

And now she was gone, the deadlock broken.

He was going to Scotland, and if his heart quit while he was there ... well, that would be Scotland's problem. And he'd meet his ancestors, be it in Heaven or Hell.

The plane broke through the clouds. Below, the land was yellow and black with a few tinges of green and dotted with houses connected by dark, shiny roads. It looked wet and dreary. Worse than Indiana.

Lightning flashed again, far away this time. Gil worked his left fist and rubbed the knuckle above his third finger where the pain started up his arm.

Schumacher laid him off after twenty-six faithful years of buying women's apparel for their downtown store. The brusque young woman in HR said they would hold his position open "because the law requires it." But his boss confided the work was being outsourced to a company in China for half what they paid him, and then mentioned an uncle who'd started drawing early Social Security.

Gil understood.

Three months later, the first check arrived the day before doctors diagnosed Clarissa with pancreatic cancer. "Inoperable," they said. She was gone in seven weeks.

He'd removed his wedding band after her funeral, but after so many years, he couldn't get used to the naked feeling and donned the silver filigree, black stone ring from his Scottish ancestors to take its place.

The pain in his arm and shoulder started that evening with the thunderstorm. He didn't expect, nor want, to survive the coming heart attack. Unemployable, untrainable, and alone for the first time in his life, Gil had no future. Just dead ancestors.

"I'm looking for *Lang Logie*," Gil said to the man with great, bushy eyebrows at the help desk. He was the only other person inside Edinburgh's poorly lit main library.

The librarian looked up from the thick book he was holding

with one hand, cocked his head and narrowed his brown eyes. "Genealogist?"

"My ancestors lived there, so I guess so." Gil grinned at the man. "I'm researching my roots."

The man shook his head. "Can't help you," he said. "Strict orders."

Gil stifled his irritation. "Do I need a library card or something?"

The man ignored him.

Gil rapped on the desk. "Excuse me! I'm not asking you to find it or anything. Just give me some ideas where to start."

The librarian exhaled and leaned over to nod. "The gazetteers behind you. First rack on the left. Nationals by year on top in green, regionals below alphabetically in red."

With that, he hunched forward into his book. Only his wavy hair showed.

At the bookcase, Gil grabbed the green spine of the top-left volume embossed with last year's number. He flipped to the *L*s but found neither *Lang Logie* nor *Logie, Lang*.

The next volume was the same. He skipped to the right end of the shelf, to the "1914" edition.

Lang Logie: A long, low place. Strathmore.

"Hah!" he jeered aloud. Across the room, the librarian's head didn't budge.

He thumbed forward to find Strathmore.

See Perthshire, it said.

"Shires are like counties, right?" he mumbled. "Need the regional now."

He put the green book away and leaned in to scan the red volumes. On the fourth row down, it jumped from Peebleshire to Renfrewshire, but with no Perthshire between. He checked every shelf.

Back at the help desk, Gil asked, "Is Perthshire checked out?"

"Reference works never leave the building," the man droned without looking up.

"Well, it's not on the shelf," Gil fired back and waved at the empty room. "And I don't see anyone who might have it."

The man's mustache twitched back and forth before he stuck a pink 3x5 card into his book and closed it.

Yanking up the handset of his phone, he jabbed three times at the button dial, then drummed his fingers until a voice squeaked from the earpiece.

"Perthshire Gazetteer," he said in a tired voice.

The voice squeaked again, and he hung up.

"Wait," he said without looking at Gil. "Michael's coming."

Picking up his novel, he rotated the chair to show Gil its back.

Across the room, a door latch clicked and a man in an open-necked white shirt and tan Dockers entered the main room. He strode over to Gil.

"Perthshire?" he asked. His tongue clicked the letter *R* and made the first syllable sound like *pear* not *per*.

Gil gave a quick nod.

Michael winked and jerked his head toward the back wall. He started walking. Gil followed.

Through the door, they entered a room that smelled of dry paper and wool with eight tables in two rows. All held books, some in neat stacks, but others were open and askew. A man in a brown, three-piece tweed suit with a blue polka-dot bow tie sat at the nearest table, his nose almost touching an open volume.

Michael called out to the room, "Perthshire Gazetteer?"

"Here."

A woman in a white blouse waved from a desk, her painted fingernails flashing white from a dim corner of the room.

Michael gestured. "Margaret will help you."

When Gil reached her desk, she used a white-tipped fingernail to push black-rimmed glasses up her nose.

"What term?" she asked, her other hand resting on a red leather volume.

"*Lang Logie*? My dad always said we came from there—our ancestors, I mean."

Her fingernails flashed as they riffled the book's pages like a stack of twenties. Near the middle, she stopped and turned the book for him.

Gil read aloud where her finger pointed. "Between Meigle and

... Glamis?"

"*Glahms*," she corrected. "Named for Lord and Lady *Glahms*. The Queen Mother, their youngest daughter, stayed in their castle when visiting. And her daughter's daughter, Queen Elizabeth II, also spent much of her childhood there with her younger sister, Princess Margaret."

"*Glahms*," Gil said, wondering why they wasted a syllable if you weren't supposed to say it.

"Mr. Dowd?" she called across the room. "Would you favor us with the Castle? Our American friend is researching his royal ancestry."

The man in the tweed suit and bow tie laid his pencil in the crease of his book before standing and walking over.

"Surname?"

"Watson. I'm Gil."

Mr. Dowd chewed the inside of his lip. "Nope. No Watts or Watsons in the Royals. Possibly in service, though." He smiled at Gil. "No offense."

"In service?" Gil asked. "You mean like in the Army?"

Margaret smirked. "In the castle. Upstairs, downstairs, you know? The staff."

Gil mouthed an "Oh" with his nod.

"The Castle originated in 1016 as a hunting lodge," Dowd began, reciting as if from a book while signaling his own observations with a glance. "Ashe's speculations, however, place King Arthur in the area late in the sixth century. Some claim that period for the dwelling's origin. Authoritative records, however, don't begin until centuries later with Malcolm II." He glanced at Gil. "As you probably learned in school, Thane Macbeth murdered Malcolm in 1034. *Glahms* was his castle."

"Macbeth? Shakespeare's Macbeth?" Gil remembered long, florid speeches and three witches stirring a pot, but high school was a long time ago.

Dowd nodded. "The castle was built in 1372 and rebuilt in the 15th century. It has undergone multiple additions, burnings, reconstructions, and enhancements over time. Much evil has been done there."

A door clicked. Gil glanced at the sound to see Michael returning with several pink 3x5 cards in his hand.

Margaret drew Gil's attention back. "There's a picture on the 10-pound note."

The airport money changer had included one. Gil took out his wallet.

"It's on the back," she said as he fished it out.

Printed in reddish ink, it looked more like a country estate than a castle. No moat or drawbridge—just an ordinary-looking front door flanked by rounded spires and stone-block roof edging.

"If you count the windows," Michael suggested, peering over Gil's shoulder, "there are more on the outside than on the inside."

Gil bunched his eyebrows wondering how that was possible.

But Mr. Dowd nodded immediately.

"The Monster. They bricked over the door to his room, supposedly a demented child. Guests say you can still hear him screaming in the night."

"A vampire," Michael said with a shrug. "To protect the neighborhood, they enticed him into a room and then sealed it up. But they say he still flies the castle halls at night to feed."

Margaret chimed in. "What about the girl screaming from a barred window?"

"No tongue," Mr. Dowd explained. "Cut out to protect some family secret. And, of course, there's the Grey Lady. They burned her, Lady Janet Douglas, at the stake for witchcraft in 1537."

Gil slowly shook his head at the horrors, the savagery, the ignorant superstitions.

Michael turned to him.

"What's your connection to the Castle?"

Gil shrugged. "My dad just said we came from the area."

Margaret held up the Perthshire book. "His Lang Logie is about two miles from Meigle on the highway. It'd be another four to the Castle."

"Could be staff," Dowd said, turning to Gil. "Any dates?"

"Dad said the 1850s."

Margaret nodded. Mr. Dowd looked pensive, and Gil had nothing more to offer.

"Very well then," Michael said decisively. "Mid-nineteenth century with a hundred-year span. Watts or Watson."

"Oh yeah," Gil added, "Dad mentioned a tollhouse."

Michael straightened.

"Margaret, let's have maps of the area. A tollhouse suggests the King's Road, probably going to the Castle, so find us the alignment. Mr. Dowd, consult the Castle staff rosters—someone living off-estate—and I'll take Meigle."

He glanced at the clock.

"Let's do one hour."

The three librarians scurried off.

Standing beside a desk piled high with books, Gil chuckled. Without asking, three professional researchers were now digging up his dead ancestors.

Margaret was late getting back.

At the desk where Gil had waited, Michael set down a page filled with lined rows. Its sharp, metallic tang suggested an ancient, wet-process copier.

"1851 Perthshire census," he explained to Gil and Mr. Dowd as he ran his finger down to a line with dense, erratic handwriting. "Here."

Gil leaned in. The writing was terrible. The two-word name started with "J" and "W" but other than being about the right length, they could have been many things other than "James Watson." His occupation of *"toll-taker"* seemed obvious, but then they'd expected it. But for some curious reason, the name of the location was a sweeping, graceful, and perfectly legible *"Lang Logie."*

Michael placed an orange book on top of the census sheet and opened it to a pink 3x5 marker.

"Meigle was a Pict settlement in AD 300," he said. "Lang Logie translates as a long, low place between two mountains. It was known well before the Angles, Saxons, and Jutes began arriving in 449 AD. They were—"

Margaret bumped Michael aside as she pushed in.

"Look at this," she said and unrolled a photocopy of a map.

"1715 survey. The Grampian Mountains are here." She swept a hand across the top, then pointed to one, then another collection of little squares. "Meigle and *Glahms*."

Holding the map in place with one hand, she jabbed a white-tipped fingernail at a spot southwest of Meigle—a tiny cross with minuscule lettering.

"Can you read it?" She grinned, but answered before anyone could look. "It says, 'Arthur's Stone'!"

Michael and Mr. Dowd both gasped.

"Isn't that—" Dowd started, leaning forward.

Michael craned his neck to read the map past Mr. Dowd's head. "I thought that was in Cornwall?"

Margaret shook her head, the grin widening. "And it's only on the 1715 map. None after that."

All three librarians spoke.

"Someone moved the stone?"

"So, the legend ..."

"How would they do that?"

"It became a farm, so ..."

"Did they bury it?"

Margaret's grin spread even wider. "This is the official map commissioned by the Crown. The map has been in the archives for centuries and people have consulted it hundreds, maybe thousands, of times. But apparently, this annotation has escaped notice."

Mr. Dowd tugged at the bows of his tie. "Well, we know he ranged up there after the Roman campaign. The stories are contradictory, of course, but ..."

"Until now," Michael whispered as he studied the map.

"I'm sorry." Gil shook his head. "I don't understand."

All three librarians were grinning. Michael said, "You found it, Margaret. You should explain."

She shook her head. "No. Mr. Dowd is our Arthurian expert. Gavin, if you please?"

Gavin Dowd bowed slightly to Margaret.

"Arthurian lore," he began, "ranges from mundane to fantastical. There are no written records from that time—Dark

Ages, you know—"

"Fifth through the fourteenth centuries," Margaret clarified under Dowd's uninterrupted oratory.

"—Geoffrie of Monmouth's account from the twelfth century is doubtful at best, and some parts are obviously made up, purely for entertainment. Overall, it's impossible to say if the Arthurian stories are about one man or several. Ashe's analysis is better, but even he admits to guesswork."

Dowd took a breath.

"But there are things repeated across the sources. First, we know there was a king named Arthur in the early five hundreds. And he left England to battle Lucius Tiberius, the Roman Emperor who demanded tribute even though Rome had abandoned Britain in 409. It'd been paid since the time of Julius Caesar—before Christ—but Arthur set out to force its termination. In his absence from England—and this is where the stories vary—he entrusted his kingdom to a cousin or nephew who usurped the affections of Arthur's queen, Guanhumara."

"I thought that was Guinevere?" Gil said. In his mind, a regal face, pale with copper hair, came into view but quickly faded when Margaret spoke.

"Same person, different traditions, different names and spellings: Guinevere, Guanhumara or Ganhumara, Vanora, Wanda ..."

"When Arthur returned," Mr. Dowd went on, "he found that Modredus—commonly called Mordred—had taken over his kingdom and stolen his wife. The armies of the two men clashed at the Battle of Camlaan. Arthur was mortally wounded, and he died soon thereafter, but not before decapitating Mordred."

Gil winced.

Michael prompted. "Now tell him the Scottish variant."

Gavin took a breath. "In Ashe's Scottish version, highlanders kidnapped Vanora—Guinevere—and her feelings changed during captivity, just like in the English version."

"The most beautiful woman in all of Britain," Michael said with a leer. "Mores were ... different then."

"In the Scottish variant," Mr. Dowd resumed, "after Arthur

returned from his quest, he went north and rescued her. But because of her infidelity, he tied her to a rock for the wolves. As for Mordred, the accounts say he was '*cut through his mailed neck as through straw.*'"

Mr. Dowd explained to Gil, "The place was called Arthur's Stone, but its exact location has remained a mystery."

Margaret unrolled another map atop the first. "This is the area today. Meigle is here on the A94 from Perth." She swept her hand to the right. "It continues east to *Glahms* and skirts the present-day castle estate."

She leaned in and moved her hand halfway back toward Meigle, then slid it a little south.

"See here? This line of trees would've been along the edges of the King's Road. You can see them here, here, and here." Her finger continued west. "If we extrapolate the alignment ..."

She stopped on a small, rectangular space down and to the left of Meigle.

Michael leaned in. "A farmer's field?"

"Probably. It's less than a mile from the King's Road alignment near Ardler. Meigle is just uphill from there, according to the terrain lines."

Michael explained to Gil. "The Meigle parish's graveyard contains Vanora's Mound. There's a museum next door with Pictish stones. One of them—contested by some experts, mind you —shows Vanora being attacked by wolves."

Gil sighed in exasperation. "This is obviously very exciting for you, but what does it have to do with my ancestors?"

Margaret grinned as she ran her alabaster fingernail up to Meigle and then a little east on the A94.

"Here."

The tip of her polished nail rested next to a rectangular outline beside the highway. In a cursive script, some cartographer had written, "*Lang Logie.*"

Gil looked back and forth between the two maps, then shook his head. "It's on the highway here, but that's not where you said the King's Road was."

Margaret leaned in to compare the maps, then creased the

paper as her nail slid down half an inch to a short line of trees. Next to it was a tiny square.

"How about this?"

Michael studied it. "A one-room stone cottage?"

"If those trees mark the King's Road," Dowd said, "that could be a tollhouse. And your Watson ancestor said he was a toll-taker. *Lang Logie* was likely the general name for the area, not any farm or dwelling."

Margaret pushed up her glasses. "They'd live by the highway so they could hear approaching riders and wagons to come out and collect—"

A voice boomed. "What's going on here?"

In the door from the main room, the help desk librarian stood, fists on hips and bushy eyebrows canted down.

Michael started brightly. "Margaret's made a discovery—"

"No!" The man cut him off as he took a challenging step into the room. The door latched behind him. "Your job is re-shelving, keeping the stacks neat, and doing research assigned by the council. That's all. Patrons must do their own work."

"They were only getting me started," Gil said, his annoyance rising again.

From the corner of his eye, he saw Michael and Margaret exchange glances.

She started walking directly toward the librarian, wiggling the fingers of her hands in a way that drew the man's eyes.

"Now, now," she said with a smile and stopped in front of him. "Let us be considerate of our American visitor. Mr. Watson isn't familiar with our rules."

Hidden from the man's vision, Michael lowered the two maps, rolled them together, and then tapped the end of the tube on Gil's thigh. Gil accepted it and turned the roll to hide behind his back.

"I have to leave now."

Gil began sidling through the desks keeping the gift hidden.

The help desk man's mustache twitched when Gil reached the door.

"Thanks," Gil shouted before the man could object and backed out.

Mr. Dowd's smirk and Margaret's gleeful grin were the last things he saw before the door closed.

The drive from Edinburgh to Meigle proved more stressful than expected. At first, it was easy because of the divided motorway, but after a few miles, he realized the slow lane was on the far left instead of the far right; he'd been driving under the limit in the fast lane which explained the angry looks from passing cars.

But the worst part came when he exited the M90 for the A94 in Perth. The smaller road was two-way, no divider, and it wormed through the middle of town. Then on the far side, the huge roundabout with one big and three smaller circles around it was the worst. He tried following another car as it threaded its way through but then had to go all the way around an extra time when he missed the sign for Meigle.

Nerves frazzled, Gil found the Kinloch Arms mid-afternoon. It looked like a house designed for a large family. His room was upstairs at the far end of a hall that stepped down in one place, then back up again. Everything had a musty, well-worn smell. He unpacked into a dresser that'd come from somebody's bedroom. The single bed looked small but had a nice, soft throw, probably from a yard sale.

The rate included breakfast which he hoped would be generous because the bill would burn up his remaining cash, depending on when they wanted payment; it might be his only meal of the day.

But then again, with the pain in his arm and shoulder worse than ever, he didn't expect to check out.

But not yet.

Out his window, the headstones of the Meigle parish's graveyard waited. Most were gray and leaning one way or another. Several lay flat on the ground. Above, a knotted layer of thickening grey clouds covered the sky. It was going to rain. And soon. Lang Logie would have to wait.

He went out the hotel and up two dozen paces to an iron gate set deep in a moss-encrusted, red stone wall. Sitting open, it admitted him to the church's packed gravel path that matched the slate of both sky and headstones. Halfway up the slope, it forked with a small sign pointing left.

Vanora's Mound.

After another twenty steps, he stopped in front of a stone set in the ground. About a foot wide, deep, and high with a sloped top, it bore a weather-pocked sign with white lettering on grey metal. Black lichen had eaten into many of the letters.

Gil leaned forward to read it out loud.

"'This mound is by tradition the burial place of Vanora or Guinevere, the legendary queen of King Arthur. The stone claimed to be her monument is now within Meigle museum at the south-west corner of the churchyard.'"

Behind the marker, the mound was just that, a mound. Maybe twenty feet across, heaped only a foot high and covered with plain grass; a few modest trees formed the back boundary. No headstone, no glass-cased sign board, nothing else promoted it.

A voice said, "She's not there, you know?"

The man was slim, a little taller than Gil, and dressed in black except for a white, twin-tailed clerical collar that fluttered with the damp wind. He had a long face, the kind that made people open their emotional floodgates and vent their frustrations.

"I'm sorry?" Gil asked.

"Only her hand is there. Her body," the man said, looking at the mound and shaking his head, "it's not there. Wild dogs, the legend says."

He smiled and offered his hand. "Jonathan Love. This is my parish."

"I'm Gil Watson." He shook Love's hand. "American."

"I know. Your accent." He folded one hand into the other as if he were preparing to lead a congregation in prayer, then cocked his head. "Doing the sites are we?"

"A few," Gil admitted. "I have a great, great grandfather from here. James Watson. Just up the road. Lang Logie?"

The minister nodded. "The farm. There's a sign on the right a few miles out. You won't have any trouble spotting it. But the owners are Paddington. No Watsons in the area. Although we could consult the registry. Would you like to come in?"

Gil waved at the marker. "What's it mean about *the stone*?"

"In the museum." Love pointed toward the back of the graveyard at a long, quarry-stone building the same color as the rain clouds. "It's closed now, but there are pictures in the guidebooks. Some say the stone depicts Guinevere being attacked by the wolves. Others say the animals are worshiping her."

Thunder rumbled.

Gil's left fist spiked with two jolts of pain. He stuck it in his pocket, hoping the warmth would help.

"Going to rain," the minister said, looking up. "Are you at the Kinloch Arms? If not, you could shelter inside."

As if fulfilling the man's prophecy, another rumble sounded closer than before.

A fresh stab of pain made Gil wince. He jammed his fist deeper into his pocket.

"Are you all right?"

"Just my arm," Gil said, massaging the shoulder. "Storms seem to make it worse."

"You should have that checked. Pain in your left arm and shoulder—"

"I know," Gil said but waved his right hand at the mound. "You said they found only her hand?"

The man paused before answering. "Only her hand is there."

Gil's eyes narrowed. Those were the same words uttered a moment ago. It was like a lawyer's statement intended to deflect attention instead of answering a question. And the chief librarian in Edinburgh treated Gil with hostility and suspicion. He'd been told the Scots were friendly, but now that he was here, and remembering the stories about the castle just a few miles down the highway, his opinion had changed.

At that moment, a powerful gust raked the churchyard. The small trees behind the mound thrashed side to side as the pastor's collar tails fluttered like mast-topping pennants.

Rain smelled moments away.

Already moving, Jonathan Love beckoned. "We'd best shelter now."

Inside the dark church, the stale smells were worse than the hotel. Recently soaked wool and people who hadn't bathed in a week came to mind.

Gil huffed at the foul air as he strode to keep up. They walked past rows of wooden pews inside the stone walls. Every five or six steps, the builders had embedded pointy-topped stained glass windows deep in the wall. They depicted saints holding staffs, lambs at their feet, with ecclesiastical signs glowing in the heavens. Overhead, the ceiling was dark with massive wooden beams and an equally dark lattice of crosspieces. Gil remembered the sheets of slate on the outside—in essence, a stone roof—and wondered at the weight over his head.

He followed the man around an altar table with candles and paused at a door.

"My office," Pastor Love said, opening the door.

Inside was a neat but sparsely furnished space. Two bookcases with dark, lacquered shelves and an old wood desk confronted a straight-backed guest chair. High in the stone wall, a small, stained-glass window, its depiction difficult to make out, gleamed with the failing light outside. To Gil's relief, the air was fresh, filled only with the scent of imminent rainfall. Caulked into a precisely cut, rectangular hole in the ancient stone wall, a small, modern air conditioner hummed and blew cool, dry air.

Pastor Love turned on a desk lamp with a green glass shade. The light added a warm glow to the ancient wood desk, but the greenish cast made the dark lichen growing in the wall's grout look like old scabs.

He opened a drawer and produced two short, crystal glasses and a half-empty bottle of Lagavulin single-malt Scotch. Mid-label, it said, "Distiller's Edition."

"Join me?"

"Um, sure," Gil answered, surprised and pleased.

Although Gil wasn't sure what to make of this man, his taste in Scotch was impeccable. The dark, gold liquid felt like velvet on the tongue with an aroma of shaggy, thick grass in fertile loam. Inhaling through nose and mouth, Gil felt like he was face down in a field that'd never been mowed. A rich, mind-filling earthiness muted his brain as the warm bloom spread from the bottom of his empty stomach.

They sipped their glasses and listened to the rain battering the little stained-glass window. It reminded him of afternoons in Indiana when storms raged through. Clarissa would be in her chair reading a romance novel from the library while he sat in his chair, holding a crystal glass and worrying about the neighbor's tree. Gigantic trees could get expensive if you didn't have someone cut away the dead parts.

The minister lifted the bottle. "Another?"

Gil nodded and set his glass to be filled. "I'm staying right here at the hotel. No worry about driving drunk."

A flash lit the room. Gil's left arm pulsed long before the thunder arrived. He began bunching and relaxing his fist in his lap.

"Outside," Gil said to get his mind off the pain, "it sounded like there was more than just her hand."

Minister Love contemplated the amber liquid in his glass for a moment, then leaned forward until his face turned green from the desk lamp's shade.

"Wanna see?"

Gil hesitated. What else had they dug up? Or had they wired the bones of her hand together like a dinosaur in Chicago's Field Museum? Flesh that had turned black from the soil? Stained, tooth-gnawed bones? A bottle of dead maggots?

"Okay," Gil said slowly, not sure of his answer.

Tilting his chair back, Pastor Love dug in a pocket of his britches and came up with a small ring of keys. He leaned forward and, from the sound of it, turned one in a drawer's lock.

Straightening up, he set a small, dark wood box on the desk. It was big enough to hold the bones of a hand, but only if stacked, one atop the next. The lid had a crack running all the way across at a slight angle. Thin, black metal straps held it together, the rounded tops of iron tacks dotting them haphazardly. A shiny brass latch, out of place with the rest of the box, had only a simple hook to hold it shut.

Pastor Love pushed the hook with his thumb and raised the lid. Inside, a triangular tongue of dark purple silk edged with gold thread covered whatever lay beneath. Using thumb and forefinger, he gently folded it back and turned the box for Gil.

Inside was a silver filigree ring with a shiny black stone.

Gil's gasp made his body jerk.

My ring!

"They say it was hers," Jonathan Love said. "Found close by."

It looked like it'd never been worn: the silver filigree had the same meticulous pattern that wove, one thread over another, for each overlapping wave. But unlike Gil's, every strand in this one stood out from the next.

Down in his lap, he snaked his thumb into his fist and felt for his ring. It was still on his finger. It felt smooth, the silver threads burnished by the thumbs and fingers of his ancestors for unknown centuries.

Two rings? He wondered.

The thought burst into his mind. *Wedding band*s!

The ring on the desk belonged to Vanora. The one on his finger, his ring, must've belonged to Arthur.

Gil took a shuddering breath.

How had it come into his family? Had one of his ancestors stolen it? Scotland certainly had thieves and murderers. He knew nothing of his predecessors. Were they tricksters? Thieves? Murderers?

Gil imagined King Arthur learning of his wife's unfaithfulness, wrenching it from his finger, and flinging it into the field where he then murdered Guinevere. The ring would then be lost to the ages, buried in the dirt for—What?—a dozen centuries until someone in Gil's family plowed it up with the season's meager potato harvest?

"I suppose," Gil said, stroking the one on his finger, "it's valuable?"

Minister Love shrugged. "It could be. They found it with her hand, but that's all we really know. It's never mentioned in any of the history books. Whether it has anything to do with Arthur, since there's no proof of any kind, is pure speculation."

Pastor Love lifted the point of the purple velvet and covered the ring. Closing the lid, he hooked the simple brass catch and returned the box to his desk drawer.

"Because of its possible provenance," he said, turning the lock, "it's protected by an Act of Parliament. You can't transfer, buy, or sell the ring. It's here for safekeeping. But with no proof ..."

He picked up the bottle of Lagavulin, tilted it toward Gil's glass, and raised his eyebrows.

Gil nodded as his mind raced.

Maybe my Watsons didn't just find Arthur's ring in some field. Maybe we had it all along, truly a "family" heirloom. For how long? Fifteen, sixteen hundred years? Passed from King Arthur to a son, to a grandson, to... how many generations would that be between him and me? How many greats?

He watched the golden fluid as it filled his glass.

I'm a descendant of King Arthur.

Gil fought back a smile.

Blood relative. I have royal blood. I am royalty.

He sat straighter, his chin higher.

Lots of people had famous ancestors, but who could say—who had an artifact, something real, that came from King Arthur?

Gil wanted to raise his hand: *I do!*

King Arthur of the Knight's Table, King Arthur and beautiful Guinevere. King Arthur and Lancelot, Sir Gawain, Percival and Sagamor, the sword Excalibur, the Lady of the Lake—

"Children?" Gil blurted out. "Did they have children?"

"Who?" the minister asked.

"King Arthur and Guine—Vanora? Did they have children?"

Minister Love shrugged. "Depends on the tradition. The Welsh say Arthur had three sons by Wanda—Guinevere—but the English say only two, and they both died young. There were others from Arthur, but not by Guinevere. And there's no mention of any by Mordred or her other crumpets."

"Mordred was a cousin?"

"Nephew," the man said, leering. "Incestuously by Arthur's sister. And a bastard, of course."

Arthur had made a baby with his own sister, with or maybe without her consent, and now this man—a priest, no less— couldn't hide his prurient titillation at their palatial bed-hopping.

Gil clenched his jaw against his disgust. This was not a man he'd want knowing his darker deeds, his failings, the awful side he kept locked away inside, the part of him that he now realized wasn't just his fault. He'd inherited it from distant ancestors, King Arthur included.

Suddenly, humans seemed like a disgusting breed, groveling and groping in the dark, mating like rats, killing and eating their own offspring.

Clarissa's decades of pouting and unprovoked rages had come from his failure as a husband. Gil's apologies, his confessions, and his promises of "never again" fell on deaf ears.

And now he understood. It was built into him. Doomed by the genes in every cell of his body, his fate was pre-ordained. There was nothing he could do about it.

Minister Love continued. "With no legitimate sons surviving, the crown and the kingdom passed out of Arthur's family after his death."

"Daughters, then?" Gil asked, wondering what would've happened to Arthur's riches. Had they been confiscated by the next King? Impounded but preserved? Did his lands pass to relatives, someone with a blood connection?

A part of his mind shouted, *Like me?*

"Legitimate or otherwise," the pastor continued, his head wagging from side to side, "the list depends on whom you listen to. There's Nathalia, Hild, one named Grega, Emaré, and nearly a dozen others with few mentions of their mothers."

Gil smirked. King Arthur certainly spread his wild oats.

King's prerogative, Gil thought. *The Divine Right of Kings.*

Mel Brooks' mustachioed leer from a movie flashed in Gil's mind. *"It's good to be the King."*

Gil glanced at the bottle of golden liquid. *And this? Is this the Pastor's prerogative? Does he buy the bottle on his own, or just take the coins from the Sunday offering?*

Gil frowned. Everybody was corrupt, vile, wretched. Some hid it better than others, but no one—at least not in his ancestry—was immune.

Light strobed in the little stain-glass window.

Gil flinched with the bolt of pain that flashed up his arm.

His ring on that finger ... it could be worth—what? Millions? Enough to buy a castle? *Glahms* Castle? Would that make him a Lord?

He could have a staff to take care of everything: a woman to cook, a gentleman to help with clothes and bathing, and girls to clean.

Or would the government impound it as property of the Crown?

The air conditioner continued to hum, but the gusts of outside air no longer pushed through. The rain had stopped beating on the stained glass.

"Sounds like a break," Gil said, keeping his own ring out of sight. "I'll head back to the hotel before it kicks up again."

"Of course," the minister said, rising smoothly. "Come back when you want to look in the church records for your Watsons."

Outside, the cold damp air made Gil shudder despite the Scotch. He focused on the edge of the path to steady his wobbly feet.

He was royalty!

Descended across fifteen, sixteen hundred years from King Arthur. The real King Arthur. And he had the ring to prove it.

He was going to be rich. Very rich.

He'd buy everything in sight. The hotel, the town, all the lands, maybe even *The Castle*.

With Clarissa gone and nothing left, dying had seemed like the next thing Gil was supposed to do.

But now ...

He grinned despite the ache of his entire left arm as he dug in his pocket for the rental car's remote. Holding it high, he pushed the unlock button. Two rows ahead, a car's lights blinked.

Mile Post Tavern was the last door in a long, white row-house with green shutters. It appeared to be the only business in the tiny village of Ardler, downhill on the narrow back road from Meigle. In the dark, the neighborhood reminded Gil's scotch-blurred brain of areas to be avoided in Indianapolis. He parked his rental car in the back after running it up the curb for a moment.

Aside from being crowded and noisy, the pub looked like someone's living room. A couch and plush seats circled a low table in the center, with small tables and chairs—none of them matching—shoved against the walls. A man with a wooden flute sat at the center table, while another dressed in kilts held a black-tubed bagpipe with copper fittings and a red tartan bag in his lap. On the couch, a woman with salt and pepper hair held a drum in one hand and a wooden spoon in the other. Next to her, a rotund man plucked two strings of his mandolin, a finger between the frets as he twisted the tuning peg. And next to him, another man silently practiced his fingering on the neck of a violin planted like a bow fiddle on his knee.

Gil concentrated on walking straight and regal as he crossed to the bar. Pump handles protruded from the counter on the barman's side with labels Caledonian, Smithwicks, and New Castle Brown.

Before Gil could order, the lady on the couch started playing a complex rhythm on her drum. Gil turned to watch. The violin and mandolin players began playing at some mutually understood cue. The flutist, however, nodded with the rhythm but kept his instrument across his lap. He raised his pint glass, finished the dark beer, then lifted it slightly to show the pint glass's condition. In the corner of Gil's eye, the barman's nod confirmed the order, and then the flute started its hop and trill. Last to enter was the hairy man in the kilt, who raised his plumbing, tucked the red, plaid bag under his arm, and began pumping. Two full strokes in, the instrument squealed like a pig seeing the knife.

When the barman looked his way, Gil tried shouting over the racket. "Scotch, please. Your best."

The man in the white shirt shrugged. He mouthed something but the only word Gil recognized was the last.

"... loud."

He blinked his agreement and waited. Long minutes passed as each musician took a turn trying to assuage the dying pig but to no avail.

When a brief silence finally returned, Gil clapped in relief with everyone else.

"Scotch," Gil tried again, pointing toward a likely bottle. "Neat."

"American?" the barman asked as he carefully filled a shot glass to its scribed line.

Gil glanced around, his eyes drawn to the piper's bare knee. The small black handle of what could only be a knife stuck up from the folded over top of the man's high, wool sock.

"Are concealed weapons common here?" Gil asked as the barman set the glass in front of him.

"*Sgain dubh*," he said. "An assassin's blade. It's a traditional part of the outfit, like his *sporran* and the Buchanan tartan."

Clueless, Gil nodded anyway.

The drummer's spoon tapped the rim twice, setting a slower tempo, and the instruments came in with the wail of the bagpipe.

"I'm from Indiana," Gil shouted at the barman. The man shrugged. Gil used his finger to trace an imaginary outline of the United States on the bar. He pointed to the state's location.

"Chicago?" the barman's mouth shaped.

"Indianapolis," Gil exaggerated in return.

The barman smiled but shook his head with a wave at the band.

Gil nodded, raised the shot glass, and tipped it in.

The liquid was fierce. It burned his tongue and his gums beneath it. He blinked, clenched his lips, took a deep breath through his nose, swallowed forcefully, and exhaled through his mouth to avoid choking on the fumes.

This was not the minister's expensive single malt. This was worse than the cheap whiskey Gil drank at home bottled by somebody in southern Ohio. There, he'd down two quick shots and wait for his regrets to dissolve and seep away, the peace of the dead taking their place. His life, the stupid choices he'd made, the consequences that'd cascaded across decade after decade, all of that would vanish.

Pastor Love's expensive booze had anesthetized him against the ripping away of his regrets, and now the pub's fiery fuel oil was burning away the ends of his emotional nerves. The prospect of never feeling anything again seemed a worthy ideal.

A banshee's screech from the violin brought him back. Looking down, his shot glass was full again.

Mercifully, the song ended, and the players set their instruments aside. Half the patrons moved to the bar for refills as others formed a line starting under the "WC" sign above a dark hall in the back.

"So, not Chicago?" the barman asked as he filled Gil's shot glass again.

Gil raised it, not remembering drinking the previous one, and turned it between two fingers, looking for a hole in the glass.

"In-di-a-nap ... o-lis," he forced his mouth to enunciate.

He flipped the newest shot back. It no longer burned, but he had to grab the edge of the bar to keep from falling backward.

"South of Chicago," he added. "Make a line down and a little east."

The barman asked, "Family here?"

"All dead." Gil laughed. "Even the King."

The flute player was standing next to him, his eyes on Gil's left hand where it held the glass. Full again.

"Interesting ring," he said.

Gil downed the shot but kept his hand up. "Family heirloom," he enunciated. "Famous. *Very* famous."

"How's that?"

"King Arthur and Guine—" He stopped and waggled his hand to erase what he'd said. "And Vanora."

The musician gave him a deadpan stare. "King Arthur? You think you're descended from Knights of the Round Table King Arthur?"

Gil blinked. "Yep."

"And you know this how?"

"King Arthur's wife. She had one, too. Same ring. Found with her hand just up the road."

The man looked skeptical but said nothing.

"I have maps."

"I grew up here," the flutist said. "I know the story."

"Well, then..." Gil said, waiting.

"Yours is one theory," he said, shifting his weight. "Would you like to hear mine?"

"Everybody's entitled," Gil said, his arm slipping off the bar. He took a moment to get it reestablished, then nodded. "Go ahead."

"The one that seems the most plausible starts with Arthur setting off with his army to fight the Romans. That's when he turned over his kingdom to his bastard son."

"Mordred," Gil supplied.

"Yes, the illegitimate son of his sister. Mordred was, therefore, also Arthur's nephew."

"I know." Gil blinked. "A bastard."

"And Vanora," the man said, "Guinevere to the English, Wanda in the Welsh tales—fell in love with him. From Mordred's perspective, since she was a legitimate queen, marrying her in that day would give him absolute authority. So, she decreed her own divorce from Arthur and then married him. That made him king, no longer just a consort."

"Better than shacking up," Gil mused, head bobbing.

"And so," the flutist continued, "when Arthur got back from Italy with his army, Mordred and Guinevere fled north and hid with Pict friends in the Highlands. They did not kidnap Guinevere, as the other story says. Instead, she and Mordred were fleeing for their lives. But Arthur caught up with them, killed Mordred, and had Guinevere executed."

Gil nodded. "Tied her to a rock. Arthur's Rock." After a beat, he corrected. "Stone. Arthur's Stone."

"If your ring is real," the flute player said, "then it belonged to Mordred, not Arthur. That would make you the descendent of a whore and a bastard, as well as a philanderer."

Blood thundered in Gil's ears.

Mordred? Mordred and Guinevere? But Mordred was King Arthur's bastard son, so I'm still related. Just not ... legally?

A man's voice echoed in his mind. *"Foul bitch. Castle whore."*

But it was King Arthur who'd slept with his own sister to make the bastard child. And all those daughters the church minister mentioned... Arthur was the philanderer, the promiscuous sower of seed, no doubt enabled by his powerful position.

Gil would have a connection, but would he still be entitled?

"That," the flutist said, pointing at Gil's ring, "can't be real. Not after all this time. It's a copy, a fake."

The reeds in the bagpipe's entrails began wailing.

The bartender's hand appeared to fill Gil's glass again.

Suddenly, he realized that everything in his stomach was going to come up. There was no stopping it.

Hand to mouth, he bolted under the "WC" sign into the back hall and just made it to the wash basin between "Lads" and "Lasses."

Outside, dark clouds hung low in the night sky. A tall streetlight made the walk, the asphalt, and even the building a bilious blue. Gil kept tilting into the side of the building as he forged his way around to the parking lot.

"Car park," he corrected himself aloud, scrambling in his pocket for the car's wireless fob.

His hotel was only a mile or two. Uphill, he remembered. Narrow lane. No traffic.

"I can do that," he said, landing in the driver's seat harder than intended.

The rain started and in moments the view was worse than through a bad piece of glass. Gil took his foot off the gas and fumbled for the wiper. He signaled a left turn, realized he had the wrong switch, over-corrected it into a right blink, found the off position, and switched to the rod on the other side. When he shoved it all the way down, the wipers swept back and forth furiously, but the deluge poured faster than they could clear.

Lightning strobed overhead. Gil's left arm and shoulder exploded in pain. He cried out and yanked that hand from the steering wheel.

The road ahead, when he glimpsed it between swipes, was a dark tunnel, a shiny black ribbon running under a long drape of trees.

Another flash lit the air. Gil's arm flinched with the pain.

"Is this it?" he wondered aloud as his car's headlights swept back and forth, lighting the trees on one side of the road then the other.

A huge clap of thunder shook the car, and to the right through the trees, a fountain of sparks spewed up pulling long, yellow flames from the ground around a brilliant dome lit from the inside. There, a streak of silver canted and swirled, glittering with blue and red sparkles.

Entranced by the flame's dance, Gil turned his head for a better view, his foot unintentionally pressing harder on the gas. He twisted in his seat to follow the scene as it began a circuit around the car. Dark trees swept across the windshield as Gil bounced on the seat trying to keep up. He stiffened his right arm on the steering wheel to push himself farther around.

Suddenly, the car vaulted up, pushing Gil hard into the seat. Then it sank, and he floated up to the ceiling. The stone in his ring flashing green, Gil held out that hand to shade his eyes from the glare.

He screamed as the car plunged in.

Black, angular shapes—trees sporting long, stiff branches with bare ends—swept past Gil's face much too close. He closed his eyes to avoid having one gouged out.

He felt the heave and thrust of a galloping horse between his legs. The animal's breathing, fast and heavy, sounded as loud as the thunder of its hooves. They raced through the nearly pitch black, Gil clinging to its back as the beast tried to keep up with another horse—Guinevere's—just ahead.

She knows the way, his mind told him.

Somewhere back there—he dared not turn to look—Arthur and his murderous band chased after them. But Guinevere knew the twists and turns of this path, and an hour had passed without hearing their pursuers.

Had they escaped?

Gil felt like he had two minds, one that was aware of his surroundings and one that recalled stories read in children's books.

Lancelot, Gawain, Galahad, Percival ... those were the names in the books. They were chivalrous and trustworthy. They fought evil, protected fair maidens ...

But now Gil knew better.

Those names, those knights supposedly in shining armor, were Arthur's goons, his enforcers, his murderers. They intimidated anyone who opposed Arthur's will, peasants and nobles alike. It didn't matter. And they killed anyone who resisted. Whole families, neighbors who witnessed something, heard something, hinted in any way... it didn't matter.

Gil remembered a quote from a high school teacher. *"History is written by the victors."*

In his day, King Arthur had been the victor. He controlled the story. His word was the only word.

Guinevere's pale face flashed back toward him from her horse. Framed in matted, reddish-copper hair, her pale skin beaded with droplets of rain—she was still beautiful.

This is a dream, Gil thought. *Not real.*

He answered himself. *But in a dream, you don't know it's a dream. So this is real, or a memory of something real.*

Guinevere pulled up unexpectedly. Gil's horse skidded to a stop.

A finger first to her lips, she pointed ahead.

The overhanging trees opened into a clearing. A small stone bridge arched over a burn—*a small stream*, Gil's mind translated—next to an open field. In its center, the dirt mounded up a few inches. Atop it, several man-high boulders shone wet in the glimmering light.

Guinevere whispered something to him. Gil felt his head nod.

He'd understood her—their sons were safe in Bordeaux now— but all her words were strange and unknown.

Sons? he wondered. *Our sons? Me and Guinevere?*

He and Clarissa never had children. His sole transgression cemented that fate.

Among the boulders, something was moving. A dark shape clambered up and turned toward them. A shiny streak of silver led by glints of blue and red lengthened at its side.

"Mordred—" Guinevere began, her wail sliding higher and the last syllable repeating, echoing, "Dread, dread, dread."

Gil clamped his eyes shut and tried to shy away, to pull back, but something was holding his elbows. He couldn't get free ...

* * *

"Stop that!" a woman's voice commanded.

He turned to look.

Navy blue V-neck scrubs revealed pale skin and the cleavage of an ample chest. A blue paper mask with red plastic glasses covered her face.

"Your arms are restrained," she said, her words causing the mask to puff out as she spoke. "Pulling is useless."

She turned to study something behind his head, then looked back down at him.

"What is your name?"

"What?" Gil shifted his body and heard the rustle of sheets. But his arms were being held, and the left one tingled like he'd been sleeping on it.

Her eyebrows rose. "Your name. Can you tell me your name?"

Gil frowned at her. "Yes."

She kept her eyes locked onto his, crossed her arms, and waited.

"Gil," he grumbled. "Galen Henry Watson."

"Good," she said. "You were in an accident, Mr. Watson, and you've been unconscious. We can't have you thrashing about and messing up the surgeon's good work."

Gil vaguely remembered plunging into a bright ball of fire with something long and shiny flickering and flashing toward him.

"I was attacked," he said.

"I see." She pushed a button on the wall behind his head. Something squeezed the upper part of his right arm.

"I was," he insisted. "Someone came at me, holding something long and shiny, a machete or a sword. It glittered. He was swinging it up and over his head. I put my arm up to ward it off …"

Gil automatically tried to raise his left arm, but it wouldn't move.

The pressure around his upper right released in little steps with clicking noises.

"Hallucination," she stated. "The anesthesia does that sometimes."

"No," he shook his head, tugging at the straps. "That's what made me crash. And then I was attacked."

She crinkled her eyebrows and frowned at a wall-mounted gauge before writing on a notepad. "One fifty-five over ninety," she said without expression.

The closest Gil had been to a doctor in the last decade was the blood pressure machine at Walmart.

"Is that good?"

"Do you take anything for high blood pressure?" she asked. "We didn't find any medications in your belongings."

"Where am I?"

She pulled a chest-high table on wheels next to the bed. A computer monitor and keyboard sat atop. She started typing and clicking.

"Royal Infirmary, Intensive Care," she said as the screen changed.

"Is that a hospital?"

She nodded. "In Perth. An ambulance brought you in from the crash." She studied the screen. "That was two days ago. You've had three surgeries on your arm. It says concussion is a concern, but you seem lucid and aware to me now. I'll update the record."

He gently tugged at both arms. "Can you untie me?"

"The right one, yes," she looked at him with an arched eyebrow, "but you have to promise not to scratch at the other."

Gil blinked and gave her his best smile.

While she unbuckled the restraint on his right wrist, he peered at the left. Two bindings tied it to the side rail, one above his elbow forcing him to that side of the bed, and the other with a pad not quite at his wrist. Beyond that, a white bandage ballooned out.

The arm was not long enough.

When she freed his right hand, he automatically reached over.

"No, no," she said, grabbing his wrist. "Don't touch."

Something was wrong with his left hand. "What've you done?"

"Mr. Watson, you must leave it alone." She pinned his right arm against the bed. "The surgeons did a good job. They said it was a clean, almost surgical amputation; they didn't have to take off much. Prepping it for the prosthetic took most of the work."

"Prosthetic?" Gil yelped and pulled. "What happened?"

"Last warning, Mr. Watson."

The leather straps and shiny buckles she'd just unfastened were right there.

Gil let his right arm go limp. "All right. I promise. Just don't tie me up again."

"You lost your left hand in the crash," she said, releasing his arm and stepping back. Watching him, she explained, "Seems you went and got yourself bladdered, then toured the countryside. No seatbelt. The report says you went through the windshield. The driver of another car saw your lights and found you in the mud. He used your belt to make a tourniquet." She paused. "He saved your life."

After a moment, she angled the computer cart so she could watch him while mousing and typing.

"He called emergency services. That's a remote area, and your car was well off the road. His name and address are in the report if you want to thank him."

Staring at the bulbous white bandage, Gil asked, "My hand?"

"Windscreen. They make for nasty cuts, but Dr. Anders said it sliced yours off square. 'Like a guillotine,' he said."

"Couldn't they sew it back on?"

She shrugged. "They couldn't find it." She pointed at a long bedside table next to his right hand. "Read for yourself. Report's in the drawer with your other things. You were in a field: mud, rain, fertilizer, all that." She gave him a disgusted look. "You wouldn't want it back, anyway. Very unsanitary. Some animal probably carried it off. A dog from the neighborhood. Or maybe a wolf down from the Highlands. They see them sometimes at Glenshee Ski Center."

"And the ring?"

"Sorry." She shook her head and pushed the tall computer cart back into a corner. "There's no mention of that. Was it a wedding band? That'd be a shame." She wore a sympathetic frown when she came back to his bed and put her hands on the side rail, one atop the other. "Is there someone we should contact? We found out from your American driver's license that you're married but couldn't reach anyone through the phone at your Indiana address."

"No." Gil shook his head, then winced at a sudden pain behind his eyeballs. "Not anymore. Just a family ring. A keepsake. From my dad."

She tilted her head to one side and smiled sadly. "Then, it's gone. Get used to it. Life's going to be different, but there are plenty of people who've lost a hand. Were you a lefty?"

"Nope." He held up his unrestrained right hand and wriggled the fingers. "Righty."

"Then you won't have to retrain much. NHS will give you a hook, but beyond that, it'll be up to you and your American Medicare. I don't know what they provide."

He stared at the bandage where his left hand should've been. "It feels like my fingers are burning."

"Phantom pain," she said. "The nerves know something's wrong, and your brain interprets it as being in your fingers."

She lifted a plunger with a black button, its cord winding back down and wrapping around the side rail. "This will add a little painkiller to the IV. Fentanyl. Good stuff but addictive. The maximum is dialed in right now. Use it when you must, but only then."

Three quick chimes sounded out in the hallway.

"That's me," she said. "If you need something, push the red Call button draped over your shoulder. Red for me, black for pain."

The police report was several pages long and included a hand-drawn map.

Near the bottom of the first page, a note said the car hiring agency would prosecute. Another one, apparently from the field's owner, explained their solicitor would seek compensation for damages not yet tallied. And the Kinloch Arms Hotel requested their billing be resolved. So did the hospital, who pointed out that the NHS billing for foreign nationals was 150 percent of standard. A final addendum said the magistrate would hold his passport pending the resolution of all complaints.

Gil knew they checked passports for international flights. Without it, he couldn't leave the country.

He sighed, tossed the report at the table, and missed. It flopped on the linoleum.

His head ached, and the fingers on his left hand burned like they were in the flame of a roaring furnace along with the hand that wasn't there anymore, the hand that lay like Vanora's in the mud of Lang Logie.

Gil whimpered once and then crushed the black button as hard as he could. Metal *clanked* behind his head, and a coolness enveloped his left arm, ran up to his shoulder, spread into his chest, up his neck, his jaw …

When Gil awoke, the first thing he remembered was the list of people who wanted money.

And that the magistrate was keeping his passport so he couldn't leave.

He came here expecting to die, but now Britain's NHS, the National Health Service, was determined to keep him alive. And they'd charge him a premium for that.

Condemned to live, the ring was his only hope.

But first, he had to find it.

The report was lying again on his bedside table. He picked it up and ruffled the pages to get to the police sketch.

Meigle connected to Glamis by the A94 that ran off the map in both directions. Ardler was farther down and had a thin line going straight up to that highway to the left of Meigle.

"The connector," Gil mumbled.

About halfway up the pencil-drawn map, a dashed line meandered across. "Mill Burn" was neatly printed above it. Beyond that, in the middle of a tree-bordered box, was an "X" with the word "vehicle."

The maps from the library, still together in a tube-like roll, also sat on his bedside table. With some effort, he separated the 1715 map, tucked the left edge under the side rail, and unfurled it across his lap.

When he compared the 1715 map to the hand-drawn sketch of

the accident, Arthur's Stone was in the same place as the X for his car.

"Hah," he trumpeted to the room, then said in a softer voice, "The ghosts. They were really there."

A different nurse bustled in. This one wore a milder shade of blue scrubs, purple running shoes, and tortoiseshell reading glasses hanging from a silver chain around her neck.

"How do you feel?" she asked, squinting at the monitors behind Gil's head. "Any lightheadedness, nausea, pain?"

"They were there," he said, shaking the unrolled survey map in his lap. "Hold this and I'll show you."

She leaned across his face to tap a gauge on the wall. "Are we feeling pain? Are we using the black button only when necessary?"

"What? No, no, I'm all right." Then he beamed at her. "My God, it was them—their ghosts, I mean. Except they were real. The sword with the jeweled hilt and all. That's what happened to my hand. I understand now."

She shook her head. "Relax, please. Your blood pressure is very high. I want you to take deep breaths. In, then out. Nice and slow."

She picked up the map and its left edge came loose. He yanked at the restraint as he grabbed for that edge with his missing hand.

"Come on, now," she coaxed, rolling up the map and setting it on the table. "We need to get that heart rate and blood pressure down. Breathe in. Deep breath."

"Stop that. I'm all right. I'm just excited because this is so fantastic!"

She grabbed his arm and clamped it under hers, the back of his forearm pressed into her breast as she felt for the pulse in his wrist.

"What are you doing?" he asked, trying to pull away.

"Just checking." Her grip, like the earlier nurse, was very strong.

"You don't understand," he argued, tugging. "I saw King Arthur. It was really him."

She kept her eyes on her wristwatch. "I see."

"He's not big," Gil said, but he stopped struggling. "Short but feisty. And filthy. Smelled like he'd been sleeping in a sewer. Not at all what you'd expect. And, boy, he was really, really pissed."

She continued holding his wrist and watching the time.

"And Guinevere—I mean Vanora, that's her Scottish name. Gorgeous, sharp as a tack, and tough."

The nurse set his arm on the bed and tucked it under the sheet when he didn't resist. "I see. And you saw them, when?"

"The night of my accident. When I lost this." He rattled the restraints on his left arm. "Arthur was going to murder her—tie her to a rock, to Arthur's Stone."

"Mr. Watson," she began calmly, "I'm sure that all seems very real to you, but I can assure you it's a false memory. You've received a lot of very strong medications. Some of them can cause hallucinations."

"No, no," he said, still beaming. "It was real." He pulled his arm from under the covers and reached toward the map again. "Let me show you."

She shook her head. "I have to get back to my station. Please practice deep breathing. In, out, nice and slow. I'll note the hallucinations in your chart. Maybe the doctor can make some adjustments."

After she left, excitement soon replaced his annoyance.

"I was attacked by King Arthur," he said aloud with a grin.

And the ring would be the proof.

A week later, he signed a sheaf of promissory notes and walked out of the hospital. But his passport remained under lock and key at the Perth Constabulary.

It was dark and raining when Gil steered another rental car over the hump of the Mill Burn bridge before stopping on the shoulder. He pulled his jacket's hood over his head and climbed out. Tucking the rented metal detector's long metal shaft under his truncated arm, he started up the incline of the road.

After two dozen paces on the pavement, he found the marks where his car must've spun off to the right. A roughly torn gap in the underbrush led through to the field.

The terrain sloped down to his right. Familiar with farmland in

Indiana, this one had been plowed across the incline to slow the drainage. Water puddled in the pebbly furrows but left the tops of the ridges soft and sticky. Following a haphazard route from one row to the next, he plodded and leapt his way to the small rise in the center.

There, keeping the metal detector still clamped under what remained of his left arm, he unwound the headphones, worked them over his head, and onto his ears. He clicked the power switch. The instrument yowled in his ears until he nulled out the sound as the man at the store had shown him.

Standing at the end of the tire tracks by the mound, he swept the detector back and forth listening for the telltale beep. He started with the area where he thought his body must have landed after being thrown through the windshield. Then he scanned both sides in case he'd rolled about. And finally, he went all the way to the far trees and back in a methodical search pattern twenty feet wide. Now and then, the device chirped, but when he re-scanned the spot, it wouldn't repeat. The dealer had said a raindrop hitting the water-proof sensor ring could do that. What he needed was a repeatable tone over the same spot.

After what seemed like hours, he'd covered most of the field but found no ring, no spare change, not even a rusty old can.

Gil sighed his frustration and looked about. The nurse said people in the area let their dogs out to roam in the evening. How large would it need to be to carry off a severed hand?

The warmth of a gigantic gray dog sprawled across his lap came to him. The animal's bony elbows pressed into the tops of his thighs, and he remembered shifting in his seat to relieve the pressure. The animal liked to snap up things tossed its way, then trot off to a safe, isolated place. Crushing the bones and turning its long head, it'd scrape out the marrow before abandoning it and cruising the raucous dining hall for another handout.

Gil wondered at the memory. He and Clarissa had cats, but never a dog. But the sense of weight and warmth on his lap was clear. He *knew* that dog.

"Tavish," he said without effort.

Tree bordered on all sides, the thicket at the bottom of the slope was densest. That copse next to the stream—*Mill Burn*—would be a good place to hide while gnawing flesh and cracking bones.

Stepping from one water-flushed furrow to the next, Gil slogged down the slope. It leveled out at the bottom, and his footing was better on the grass and twigs where the trees began. But once in, they blocked the remaining light. Sweeping the metal detector between the nearly invisible trunks, around the wild bushes, and through long grass would take forever.

A few steps ahead, he could hear water babbling. If some animal, chewing on the fingers, had spat out the tasteless, inedible ring, it might've rolled it into the stream. And the end of the metal detector was waterproof, he'd been assured. "Necessary around here," the man at the rental store said.

The stream-bottom would be an easier search.

Gil stepped down and into the icy water, and then pressed the metal detector's round sensor to the bottom. He swished it slowly across the narrow stream and worked his way downstream. After several minutes, the flow widened and deepened several inches. He guessed the bridge impeded the flow in heavy downfalls and made a natural pool there.

He jumped when the detector chirruped on the next sweep.

He swept the detector across the same stretch of pebbles, and the swooping pitch repeated, loud and insistent. He shortened the sweeps until the detector sang a steady pitch. He pressed the detector down to fix it on the spot, then planted his feet in a "V" against the edges of the sensor. The exact spot bracketed between his water-filled shoes, he brought the detector up, clamped it under his left arm, and bent forward to scrabble in the water. Most of the smooth stones were the size of a walnut—too big— and he cast them aside. What he needed would be smaller, and it'd be hollow.

In a cleft between three larger stones, his forefinger found one with a hole. He pushed his finger in. It went on to the first joint without effort.

"My ring!" His voice reverberated in the hollow beneath the stone bridge.

Afraid he might lose it, Gil closed his fist, the forefinger tucked into the center. He straightened, and once he was sure of his balance, he carefully opened his hand. The glimmer of starlight through the clouds and trees was enough to show something shiny with a big black spot in the middle.

"Yes!"

Closing his fist again, Gil vaulted noisily upstream to find a gap with no trees on the bank. He propped his butt on soggy grass, swung up his legs, rolled onto his knees, and finally stood upright in the dark.

Shoving his way toward the glimmers of light reflecting in the bottoms of the plowed rows, he was out of the copse in four steps. He slogged up the field's slope, stepping from mound to sticky mound, the mud clung to his shoes and his footing became as precarious as walking on ice.

"Better put it on right," he said, stopping just below the rise.

But, one-handed in the dark, that was not easy. After several gyrations and from the effort, he turned his hand so the ring's black eye pressed against his pants. Then, stroking it down the leg of his pants and pushing on the inside with his thumb, it slowly crept up.

The instant it bumped over the last knuckle into place, a bolt of lightning exploded directly behind him.

In the deafening silence following the thunderous clap, he felt more than heard something crackling and snapping behind him. Turning to look, he had to raise his hand against the glare. As it came up, his squinted eyes tracked the ring's stone that now glowed with a deep, murky green like a deep well with something waiting, something hidden at the bottom.

Shifting his focus through the gaps in his fingers, a scintillating hemisphere shivered atop the ground, its surface rippling with translucent waves.

And inside, something moved.

His eyes adjusting to the brilliance against the dark Scottish night, he started to see it was a woman in a long, red dress leaning against a boulder. Long, copper-colored hair dripped with rain and trickled down strong, Roman features on a pale face. A rope bound her ivory shoulders back against the rock and returned across her midriff, then her thighs, with a final pass above her thin ankles. In the watery mud, long toes clenched and relaxed as if trying to creep away.

A second figure, this one kneeling, had its back to Gil. It was a man. He wore a heavy, elegant robe, the hem brown with mud. Next to him, a shiny, metallic headpiece sat on a rock the size of a pillow. Rivulets of rain streaked the silver. The figure tugged at the ropes around the woman's ankles to cinch them tighter. She grimaced but made no complaint.

Gil straightened, but the shifting weight made his foot slide into the mud. He waved his right arm to keep from falling.

The woman's eyes rose toward the motion, searched, and found Gil's.

Relief flooded her face.

"Mordred!"

At the name, the kneeling figure bolted upright and wheeled around, his hand reaching for the jeweled hilt of the sword at his waist.

It was him. The man from the dining chamber. Arthur.

He bellowed like an outraged elephant and drew his blade. Stepping forward and baring his teeth, King Arthur raised his battle sword, the tip weaving in a small figure-eight.

"*Cut through his mailed neck as through straw,*" the librarian had said.

"I'm not Mordred," Gil shouted in the rain, putting up his only hand as a shield and taking a step back in the squishy mud.

Arthur advanced, the dome of light coming with him. The battle-marked blade glinted as its tip moved back and forth. Jewels in the hilt flashed red and blue where they weren't covered by the man's hand.

"I'm not Mordred," Gil repeated. "My name is Gil Watson. From Indiana."

But Arthur yelled again, water and spittle flying from his lips, the words incomprehensible.

"I don't understand," Gil pleaded, stepping back from the sword and having to suddenly lurch to keep his balance in the muddy field.

"My English," Gil guessed, "It's not your English."

The blade of the sword shifted a little to the side and then Arthur lunged with the blade sweeping across the same level as Gil's neck.

But Gil was already falling with one leg splayed out behind him, its footing lost, as he yanked the metal detector from under his arm and raised it for protection. At the same moment, his left arm, now freed from its duty, rose automatically to ward off the glinting blade.

It whizzed past the end of Gil's arm in front of his face and sliced through the detector's aluminum tube as if made of butter. The circular plastic end of the device flipped away with two inches of metal shaft still attached.

Where the blade had passed the end of Gil's upraised arm with the bandaged end, the gauze now flapped loose.

"Gah!"

But Arthur continued advancing, the sweep of his circling blade coming closer and closer.

Gil scrabbled backward in the mud and frantically jabbed the only thing he had, the sliced-off remnant of the detector's metal shaft.

Arthur laughed aloud as he easily dodged the amateurish thrusts.

From the rocks, Guinevere screamed something, her words like Arthur's, foreign and cryptic.

Arthur turned to her and bellowed.

She screeched back with a murderous hatred.

Arthur raged again, their furies ascending a staircase.

Gil recognized the anguish. He'd heard it in Clarissa's screaming, in her vicious, hateful tirades against his betrayal. In one moment of animal lust, Gil had failed her, and the wound, when she found out, was deeper than anything he could ever heal. In an instant, her love transmuted into hatred. Annealed stronger and more hate filled each year, she would stay, she said, to make him pay for ruining her life.

But these two, Gil realized as he watched Arthur and Guinevere screaming at each other, suffered even worse. Because theirs was not a one-way hatred from a single indiscretion, both had indulged their animal lusts, over and over, to spite, to outdo each other. And not in guilt or secrecy but flaunted for everyone to know.

"Don't you see?" Gil shouted at them, the ring on his finger glowing brighter. "You, Arthur. You are the great King, but you abandoned her, a young woman, a beautiful woman. You gave her power and authority to rule as she wished. And then you left. Two years. You ignored her for two long years."

Gil wiped the water from his forehead, his ring beaming a strong, steady green light.

"My God, man," Gil yelled, shaking his head, "your own sister? Just look at what you did, your wanderings, your lusts, your trespasses. What example did you set? What norm did you establish? How could you expect anything different from those around you? You were a leader, but where did you lead her?"

Arthur was watching, seeming to listen, somehow. Comprehending?

"Mordred," Gil started, "You—"

Arthur exploded. "Mordred!" And charged.

The stone on Gil's finger suddenly brightened into a blinding green.

Eyes squinted; Arthur lunged.

Gil automatically thrust his arm and the detector's severed shaft.

Silence fell.

Lit completely in green, Arthur stared down at the shiny aluminum shaft where it had entered his side through a seam in his chain mail.

Shocked, Gil yanked it back.

Blood gushed, black in the green light, and began coursing down the links of Arthur's armor.

Guinevere shrieked, her eyes flicking from Arthur to Gil and back.

Arthur's hideous death sentence, to abandon this beautiful woman to the wolves that would rip her body apart, fight for each arm, leg, shard of skin, each bloody organ and devour her pale body in the starless night, and then continue, to gnaw and scatter her bones...

Gil's rage overwhelmed him.

"You!" he shrieked and jabbed.

His weapon, the shaft of the metal detector with its end lopped off to a razor-sharp point, found the same gap a second time. But this time, Gil was on his feet, and the blind rage filling his mind, he stepped forward, advancing on Arthur, and pushing his weapon deeper and deeper inside the man's body. Gil felt the scrape of bone through his fingers, the resistance of some organ in his arm and pushed harder until the skin of some internal organ gave way. Stopping only when he was close enough to smell rotting teeth, the shaft of the aluminum metal detector quivered in Gil's ring-bearing hand with the fluttering of Arthur's heart.

The King, his mouth and eyes equally agape, began to step back.

Gil let go.

The metal detector's control box looked like it was glued to Arthur's side as the man staggered back.

"You made your choices," Gil screamed empty-handed while shifting his eyes between Arthur and Guinevere. "Your actions," he cried to them both, "your consequences."

Blood spurted between and around Arthur's fingers where they clamped to his side. He crumpled to his knees, looked up at Guinevere, saw her face filled with horror and sorrow, and raised his bloody hand for a moment.

He fell forward.

Dead in the mud.

A flash of pure green erupted straight up, the clouds opening to let it pass.

When Gil looked down again, blackness had returned.

A cold, ragged wind tore at his face as if to sweep the final remnants away. The trees swished and creaked. Branches clattered in the dark as, overhead, the clouds raced north up and over the Grampians and leaving an utterly clear, star-filled sky.

On Gil's finger, the black stone of his ring sparkled, the glints a deep green but a different shade now, more like that of a new seedling, of something born anew. Its past unknown, the healthy green of something ready to try again at life.

The bartender at the Mile Post Tavern grinned and reached for the Scotch.

Gil waved him off. "Club soda tonight." He gestured at his left arm in explanation, the gauze still dangling.

The bartender gawked. "I'll get my kit."

Pulling a red box from behind the bar, the man clipped off the loose end and wound fresh gauze over the stub. Tying off the end, he said, "I thought about you when you staggered out that night, but you said the hotel was ..."

Gil nodded. "It's okay. My fault, not yours."

He sat at a table well back from the band this time, the musicians obscured by the crowd standing around. There was a singer this time, a woman he couldn't see for the crowd with a high, pure voice.

Gil couldn't catch the words, some foreign language he guessed, but the sorrow and loneliness in her voice came through. He closed his eyes and let it draw out all the sadness and regret of his life.

And when it was gone, he heard inflections in her voice that promised resolution, of hope, of accepting life's mistakes, and then moving on.

Let the dead go, he thought. *Life is for the living.*

The song ended.

No one spoke for several seconds.

Gil opened his eyes to discover a woman pulling out a chair to sit at his table. She was close to his age but with the beauty of her youth shining through. Her complexion and features reminded him of the pictures of finely etched Roman statues. She wore her hair, mostly grey, in long, flowing curls. But when she turned her head and the lights in the bar hit it just right, it glinted like polished copper.

"From your expression," she said, "I was sure you understood my Gaelic."

She offered a pale hand. "I'm Wanda. From Wales."

"Galen Watson," he replied, marveling at her blue-green eyes. "Indiana."

Keeping his hand, she turned it and looked down.

"Nice ring."

www.ingramcontent.com/pod-product-compliance
Lightning Source LLC
Chambersburg PA
CBHW022054170626
46808CB00003B/1472